PINKFONG: BABY SHARK AND GRANDMA'S MAGIC WAND
A CENTUM BOOK 978-1-912841-92-9
Published in Great Britain by Centum Books Ltd.
This edition published 2019.
1 3 5 7 9 10 8 6 4 2

Copyright © 2019 Smart Study Co., Ltd. All Rights Reserved.

Original Korean edition first published by Smart Study Co., Ltd.

This edition published by Centum Books Ltd in 2019 by arrangement with Smart Study Co., Ltd.

Centum Books Ltd, 20 Devon Square, Newton Abbot, Devon, TQ12 2HR, UK.

books@centumbooksltd.co.uk

CENTUM BOOKS Limited Reg. No. 07641486.

A CIP catalogue record for this book is available from the British Library.

Printed in China.

pinkfong

BABY SHARK
STORYBOOK SERIES

Baby Shark
and Grandma's
Magic Wand

Centum

Baby Shark Family & Friends

Baby Shark

Baby Shark is curious about everything under the ocean. He likes singing as it helps him to be brave.

Mummy Shark

Mummy Shark has no limits to what she can do. She always listens to Baby Shark and shares a special bond with him.

Daddy Shark

Daddy Shark is a strong and mighty hunter. More than just a father, he also plays with Baby Shark like a friend.

Magic Wand

The magic wand is Grandma Shark's source of magic. She has to be very careful with it.

Grandma Shark

Grandma Shark likes reading. A kind and thoughtful grandma, she always has time to spend with Baby Shark.

Grandpa Shark

Grandpa Shark is wise and smart. He is famous for his hot clam buns and enjoys sharing his cooking skills with Baby Shark.

'I'm Grandma Shark of the ocean and beyond!
I can do anything with my magic wand!'

Doo-doo-doo-doo-doo, doobracadabra!

Doo-doo-doo-doo-doo, doobracadabra!

'Boo-hoo, please find my mummy.'

'I need a comfortable sofa!'

8

'My dear baby, there you are!'

'It's so soft and comfy!'

'Grandma Shark, you are the best!'

'Thanks a lot, Grandma Shark!'

Grandma Shark is so happy
that she twirls her magic wand!
But it slips from her grasp and falls
to the ocean floor.

'Oh no! My magic wand broke when it fell.
Can I still cast a magic spell?'

Just then, a bored Baby Shark swings
by Grandma Shark.
'Grandma Shark, please turn this ball into a friend.'

'Hmmm. Well, I'll give it a go.
Beach ball, bouncy and free.
Baby Shark's friend you will be!'

Doo-doo-doo-doo-doo,
doobracadabra!

What happened?
Grandma Shark turned Baby Shark
into a plush toy!
'Oh no! I must turn him back right away!'

Alive, alive, not a plush toy!
Baby Shark is a real boy!
Doo-doo-doo-doo-doo,
doobracadabra!

Ta-da!

The magic wand sparkles and twinkles!

Phew, it worked!

It's a good thing Grandma Shark knows her magic!

'I am so sorry, my dear Baby Shark.'

'No need to say sorry, Grandma Shark.

I had a blast!'

This time, Mummy Shark needs the magic
of Grandma Shark.

'This pencil stub will not do! Grandma Shark
please make it long again.'

'Hmmm, I sure hope the magic wand works
this time.'

Magic wand, you are so strong!
Make this pencil stub really long!
Doo-doo-doo-doo-doo,
doobracadabra!

Oh, no! The pencil stub got even shorter!
Grandma Shark immediately tries again.

Pencil, pencil, not a stub! Longer, longer, like a club! Doo-doo-doo-doo-doo, doobracadabra!

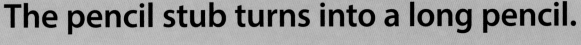

The pencil stub turns into a long pencil.
'I can use this pencil for a long time! Thanks.'
says Mummy Shark.

Grandma Shark thinks of a fun surprise
for Baby Shark!
'Baby Shark, let's make a sandcastle together.'
After they build a nice sandcastle,
Grandma Shark casts her spell.

'Sandcastle, sandcastle, ziggity-zig!
We want this one extra big!
Doo-doo-doo-doo-doo,
doobracadabra!'

'Grandma Shark! Our sandcastle is getting smaller and smaller… and even smaller again!'
'Don't worry, little one. I'll get it right this time!'

'Sandcastle,
Now it's time to
Doo-doo-doo-doo-doo,

sandcastle, oh so small!
grow very tall!
doobracadabra!'

As soon as Grandma Shark casts another spell, the sandcastle gets bigger and bigger and bigger…

Now Baby Shark has the biggest
sandcastle in the world!
Isn't Grandma Shark the best?

Grandma Shark loves her magic wand.

30

Baby Shark loves Grandma's magic wand too!